MY TUSSLE
WITH THE DEVIL

MY TUSSLE
WITH THE DEVIL

AND OTHER STORIES

By

O. HENRY'S GHOST

Short Story Index Reprint Series

BOOKS FOR LIBRARIES PRESS
FREEPORT, NEW YORK

First Published 1918
Reprinted 1971

INTERNATIONAL STANDARD BOOK NUMBER:
0-8369-3926-3

LIBRARY OF CONGRESS CATALOG CARD NUMBER:
72-160947

PRINTED IN THE UNITED STATES OF AMERICA

The Barrage Fire

 FEEL I cannot give O. Henry's Ghost better ammunition with which to meet his critics than a bit of truth voiced by Joan in one of Algernon Blackwood's wonderful books.

"The beloved dead step nearer when their bodies drop aside. They know where they are and what they are doing. It's not for us to worry —in that way. And they are *out of hours and minutes.*"

To meet the onslaught of you, Mr. Scoffer and Mr. Skeptic, who will say, "Impossible! They are not a bit like O. Henry's stories! They lack all his virility, etc., etc." I say at once, of course they are different! Where before his stories were written in the bold black and red of human passions, which belong to materiality,

3

now, they must of necessity be pastel in hue and delicate gossamer things, for O. Henry's Ghost is using finer material to mold his creations. The land where he dwells is subject to a different rate of vibration, and as the rhythm must be totally unlike, it is natural that the thoughts should flow and take form in the vehicle of poets.

But one characteristic is dominant still—the completeness of each Pastel. Not a word more is needed to complete a picture or convey an emotion, and while the aspiration of O. Henry's Ghost has changed and he deals with higher, finer forces and desires, he still retains his mastery of the short story.

Attack from all sides, if you will, but the only guns you can fire are, "I believe" and "I think," which shall bring forth in reply the bomb "I KNOW!!"

Because the spirit known as O. Henry came before the curtain on this particular stage in the garb of heavy woolen materiality, thundering vivid, scarlet tales, is no reason why, having made his exit,—after playing out his role,—he should not return in a different characterization and in chiffon garb.

If he is not recognized in the new one upon his entrance it is no evidence that the same spirit does not animate both, and the perfection of detail and artistry in both characterizations is convincing proof of the same dominant spirit.

While the stories necessarily reflect in their style the high aspiration that prompted them, they prove, as O. Henry's Ghost so vividly remarked, that a leopard can change its spots.

Flashes of the O. Henry who wrote "The Man About Town" are found in the bits of personal conversation from O. Henry's Ghost, and the old and new are blended in the following birthday greeting: "I give you my gladsome wish for a comrade and gratitude for opening the doors to a scrivener. If it was the olden days I should have been foolish enough to say 'Have a drink to celebrate.' Now I shall tell you to take a whiff of ambrosia fit for gods and shall join you with a gladsome spirit. Here's how!"

The sledge hammer blows wielded by the personality of O. Henry can only dull to insensibility and bring forth a murmur of "I think" and "I believe," while the darting shafts of O. Henry's Ghost will pierce the clouds and bring forth the chorus of "I know" to those who, having eyes —see—and having ears—hear!

It is today the same as when Plato said:

"Strange times are these in which we
                live, forsooth:
When old and young are taught in
                Falsehood's School!
And the one man who dares to tell
                the Truth
Is called at once a 'Lunatic' and 'Fool.'"

But at any rate, they go forth at the request of O. Henry's Ghost and with the belief that the beauty of thought will be a joyful remembrance of one who was known as O. Henry.

PARMA.

June 27th, 1918.
158 Ocean Boulevard,
Atlantic Highlands,
New Jersey.

Contents

Comments

Comments

THE COMING OF THE STORIES

ROM the first we used the Ouija Board not as a toy, but as a serious medium through which we received guidance in our affairs and teachings of the Great Law of Life, for which we were searching. We were determined to have only the truth, and so we eliminated the frivolous and deceiving, who are ever on the watch for the ignorant user of the "Board" —to amuse themselves with his credulity, or through sheer devilishness to lead him to disaster—material and spiritual.

Those with whom we talked were Great Invisible Teachers—who were on the Earth plane to help humanity —and a close relative whose development we followed with intense interest, and to whose advice in critical moments we owe much.

This was the situation when early in September, 1917, we were told that if we would sit at the "Board" each afternoon about four-thirty o'clock, with a positive determination to receive only that which was worth while, and shut the door at once to anyone whose offerings did not reach a high standard, we would receive things that would surprise us.

Accordingly, on September 18, 1917, we waited results—they came as follows:

"My little talent I suppose you will consider insufficient."

"Who are you?" we asked.

"Useless to give name," came the answer. *"If you do not know when the story is finished, it is N. G."*

"I wish to tell the world what is theirs for the asking. To try and

*give them a new viewpoint in place
of their erroneous ideas."*

*"I did not know as much then as
I do now. Before I wrote what the
Self saw only—now it is what I
know."*

"We'll take a chance—go ahead,"
I said.

Then followed a story called "The
Contest."

How do we know it was the spirit
of O. Henry? We will let the rec-
ord speak for itself. The truth always carries conviction, except to
minds the doors of which are double-
barred.

It was evidently the first time this
Spirit had used a Ouija Board, for
he was not sure of the location of
the letters, and after the first para-
graph said:

*"My force is insufficient; it tires
me to spell each word so slowly."*

We told him to go as fast as he

liked. He soon learned how to apply his force, and all went smoothly.

When the story ended, I wrote the name *"O. Henry"* on a slip of paper and asked if I had guessed correctly. The reply was *"Yes."*

We were so impressed with the story that I said, "It is good enough for the Atlantic Monthly."

The comment was, *"If they take it, my revenge would be complete. That is for the 'Elite,' I did not belong."*

The next day came first what was evidently a title, *"My tussle with the Devil."*

We asked, "Who is speaking to-day?"

"An imaginative fellow," was the reply.

"Is it the same with whom we talked yesterday?" we asked. *"Yes; it is a joy once more to weave a plot."*

A little later, when the work was resumed after an interruption of several days, O. Henry's Ghost began with:

"I am glad to see you."

"Did you miss us?"

"That's what!" was the answer.

The day was rainy and the story rather serious, or so it impressed us, for we asked:

"Why don't you give us a cheerful story?"

His reply silenced further suggestions. It was:

"Kindly allow me to express what I feel."

O. Henry's individuality was clearly marked from the first and we had no doubt about his genuineness, but an incident which occurred one afternoon may serve to convince the skeptical.

Several times we had been bothered by the interruptions of a boy Spirit called William Mumm, who was possessed with an over-developed sense of humor. Often we knew that O. Henry was being crowded by others who thought that they should be given a chance to express themselves, and once or twice the writing stopped until things quieted down. On this occasion Mumm broke in with, "Henry is giving too many orders."

On being told in a forceful way what we thought of his interference, he said, "My word! That was a hot shot! I won't butt in again:"—and he didn't.

Later, when we asked O. Henry whether others were present, he said, *"They are hanging around, but not butting in."*

As we got better acquainted, there was more conversation of a personal nature before the story for the day was started.

To the question whether before he "crossed over" he had had any real Truth, he said:

"No, my teaching was hell and damnation."

We, of course, were curious to know how he discovered us. His answer was in line with what we had been taught—that each person appears as a light, shining with increasing brilliancy as one learns the Truth and lives it. He said:

"Letting your light so shine led me here—I desired to tell what I felt and knew, and sought an avenue; your beacon beckoned me, and your teacher bade me enter."

Once when we mentioned a financial pressure he said:

"That's the only hell there is on earth—that and lack of love which sends one to rum shops."

After another break in our work with the stories, we were welcomed with:

"It has been a long time since we have talked. I wish you joy."

To our usual question "who is with us?" came the answer:

"I was called Henry."

A glimpse into conditions on the "other side" was given when we asked O. Henry whether he had found a friend of whose "passing over" we had told him.

"No," he replied; *"I have not found him. He must be resting, and we make it a point never to disturb, for the rest periods are of the most importance and hasten growth. I shall watch for him when he makes his mansion."*

"What do you mean by that?" we asked.

"In the beginning of life here we make little progress—unless knowledge of the Truth has been ours before coming over. That is why it is so necessary to learn before leaving the Earth Sphere. Without that one must wander aimlessly or rest

and gaze at things of the past—and
our associates are other unfortunates
who have had closed ears before leaving.

"When one has reviewed a certain
number of lives—or generally a se-
quence of events—then comes a tender friend who points out advantage-
ous work and study, and which, if
followed, always means the beginning
of progress and growth. It is only
after that has been made use of that
we begin our mansion or abiding
place.

"Keep it always in your mind, the
foundation stones are Knowledge,
Wisdom, Power—and then it is built
by the thought and desire of Aspiration, Beauty and Love.

"I want to impress upon you and
all mankind the necessity of 'Knowing,' and, what is more to the point,
'Believing.'

"If you will lend me your pencil,

*most generous person, I may be able
to say all I want. Now it seems
as if I never would be able to get rid
of it all.*

*"If you would publish a magazine
it would be a 'hummer.' The trouble
is, there is no periodical which has
any one back of it who KNOWS.
They all prattle and the almighty dol-
lar is the main thing. Truth would
bring them faster than anything if
they would only believe it.   Let's
work it out! It would be great! Now
to work, if you don't mind.*

*"In a sunny nook by a babbling
brook I have built my mansion."*

O. Henry was very enthusiastic
over the idea of a magazine.   Refer-
ring to it again, he said, *"Call it the
Sphinx."   Get at it at once.   Have it
contain only tales which teach, and
Wisdom."*

Once when he talked on until late
in the evening, and we became tired,

he said, when the lateness of **the hour** was mentioned:

"It is all the same here; I forget. My impatience is still that stumbling block. With many thanks—good night."

One rainy day we were **ready** earlier than usual and O. Henry was evidently in exceptionally good humor, greeting us with:

"Well, this is a surprise! It's bully!"

"Kind of nice in here. We do not feel the rain, but we like sunshine better."

One story we received was **not up** to the O. Henry standard, and **we did** not hesitate to say so. Our **views** must have been rather more forcefully expressed than we realized, **for** he said:

"I have read and had many criticisms of my stories before, but they never came as hard or as fast as this one. Wipe it out."

With that he redictated the last half of the story, changing it completely and to the satisfaction of all.

With his next story we were particularly pleased, and on our saying so, he said:

'I thank you and am glad you really like it. Have to watch my P's and Q's now or I will lose my publisher. It is great to be compelled to do one's best. It means the continuation of aspiration. Lying Spirits do not aspire. Having publishers who will accept nothing but the truth and only the best one is capable of is a bit of a novelty. Pity there are not more of them for material, as well as spiritual fiction. You might get Hoover to add that plan for conservation of paper and ink. If we over here had more publishers like you there would be more truth spread broadcast. The trouble is most of the offices accept anything, just so it has a name attached.

"What's in a name?—Nothing."

"What's in a Truth?—Every-
thing."

Unless the Spirit moving the indi-
cator on the board is an advanced
soul, having great power, he usually
draws from the persons he is work-
ing through. This O. Henry was at
times forced to do, and so we under-
stood, when one day, instead of starting a story he said:

"Your teacher says you hesitate to
tell when you are tired. Better to
have a perfect pen for two lines, than
none at all for twenty. Tell me the
moment you become fatigued. There
is time for the lot. If you are de-
pleted through my coming, it will be
curtailed, if not stopped, and that
would be too dreadful! Much better
a half a loaf at a time than none at
all. Please tell me. Your teacher
thinks you have sufficient without
what I am dictating, but feels that it

is worth while providing you are not in any way injured by the work. I so want to have the opportunity. Do, kind person, tell me and let us go slower. Last night I chattered; no reason for it at all, except the pleasure of doing it, and you were tired, the teacher says, before I began."

We agreed to be more careful, and O. Henry said:

"That's a bargain."

In speaking of the many plots crowding his mind and which he wanted to express, he said:

"Riches are a burden at times. I wish to rid myself of them. Quick returns will follow. With much material off my mind I shall be able to develop much, more worth while. Hurry! Life takes up so many hours."

Before starting a series of stories of a different nature from those given first, he said:

*"My wish is to widen the horizon.
It is important for humanity to
know. It must recognize the oneness
of everything. We will write of
more than man. I will give a series.
First Beasts—then Flowers and
Jewels."*

When these stories were completed,
everything seemed to conspire to pre-
vent the devoting of a quiet hour to
O. Henry and his stories. Whenever
constructive work is done, by which
the Truth may be brought to many,
the forces of destruction are arrayed
in opposition. This we felt to the full.
Twice stories were started and
stopped after only a few paragraphs
had been written. In one it was evi-
dent that O. Henry had been pushed
aside and a complete sentence injected
by some "Power of Darkness." We
at once realized the situation and put
the "Board" away.

When next O. Henry came, he
said:

"The time has been long. Why keep the Muse silent? I am simply overburdened with plots."

When asked the cause of the breaks in the last story he said:

"I find there are still a number of people who believe they know better how to write my stories than I do.

This last time it was 'Fiends.' It is important you keep the door closed by demanding you receive only the truth—for that prevents their taking definite hold."

About this time there appeared in the papers notices of moving pictures made from the O. Henry stories. We asked him what he thought of them, and his answer, concise as usual, was:

"Foolish rehash of yesterday's ignorance."

In commenting on how few believed and how difficult it would be to find a publisher, O. Henry answered:

"My belief is you will have to do it yourself ultimately, if you cannot find some one who is independent. The trouble is that in a concern, one may believe, while the rest of the company do not yet see."

The conditions of everyday life became worse. We were able to snatch only a few minutes with O. Henry and asked him if he felt the confusion.

"It is a regular whirlpool, he said; *the boat rocks. Until you can have quiet I think it would be wiser to postpone trying to write. My wish is added to yours, for if all disturbance is eliminated we can then accomplish a great deal without effort."*

On New Year's eve we received greetings from those with whom we had been closely associated in work, and last of all came O. Henry. He said:

"I do not belong, but I may come to the party, may I not?

"I am content to wait until it will be only a pleasure to hold converse and when we can relax to a real confab.

"They are good stories, if I do say it—but they cannot believe in a leopard changing his spots. Out upon that spot!

"An amazing thing that the stolid English are more awake spiritually than Americans, who have not yet been touched vitally. Some day they will awake and arise—and I hope then I can take part in the procession.

"My greetings and all aid possible for the year to come."

Several weeks later he said:

"This is the first opportunity I have had to hold 'mind' with you.

"Interesting expression that, when one realizes how true it is that mind is the only real point of contact, although when on your plane we speak

only of · the physical nearness of others.

"Is it true that the hour is to be re-established? If that is the case, we ought to turn out something worth while."

On being told that the poem, "Sleeping," which he had given us, was to be read to the Poetry Society, it seemed to appeal to his sense of humor, for he said:

"If I was not to all appearances dead, that would be my death. I shall have a fearful attack of stage-fright. I do hope they won't call 'Author!'

"I like this house. It is so restful and harmonious. It is a smiling island of loveliness in a black sea of pitch. I shall stretch here at ease tonight and rest and live happily."

A. HOUGHTON PRATT.

"Over There"

O. Henry's Ghost Answers the Questions of a Newspaper Man Regarding "Over There"

SO he desires to know how we folks live?

Queer! the idea humanity hugs to its breast of how different life must of necessity be over here.

Tell him that at present it is New York at its worst, on a day of celebration,—with streets crowded, people pushing in all directions, friends meeting, exchanging greetings and passing on. To us life is the same, with the exception that now time is no longer a factor.

Our emotions are the same—until we learn the wisdom of eliminating all unworthy ones.

33

Our desires the same—only now they are satisfied almost immediately. We desire to eat and we have food. All is the same, only of finer material, not so dense.

It is as if we were in airships above you—seeing all, comprehending all, and yet unable to make you hear. To the few are given ears attuned to hear and eyes which behold, but humanity as a whole is blind.

If you could by any method make the world realize that to us *here* each and every THOUGHT affects us more poignantly than all the sentences uttered and that we are uplifted and made joyous by each thought of love sent out, *no matter to whom,* all hate would vanish from the earth.

Clothing? Just the same as ever, only we are glad to discard the old garments for new ones more beautiful, after we have been here for a while, and when that desire comes, the material is at hand with which to create new garments. Verily, over here thoughts become things quickly.

There are those here who do not aspire for newer or better things, and so they remain in their same condition.

Aspiration is the force here which pushes you on to better and greater achievements

Houses? Certainly we have them; each one to his liking, for he builds it as he desires, with the aid of others; all lend helping hands over here, and life becomes a proper mixture of work, play and study.

Yes, there are places where hate, envy and all the evils still hold sway, and if those are the things which you enjoy, you dwell in that locality.

Whatever you in your soul desire you receive. Ask and it is given you; seek higher and you find; and it is truly to be said: "As a man thinketh so he receives and is."

Naturally, people of the world are going to say: "O. H. cannot write from above—if what he says is true, he would be below." Having spent several years in Hell—on earth—after I arrived in this country I was mighty glad to change my environment when I discovered where I had been dwelling,—and that there was no need of remaining, unless I wished,—so I gave notice to the landlord I was moving at once.

The earth is a pretty poor place when you make a hell out of it, and it might be a heaven if we would only have faith, love and aspire.

The world is on a precipice and New York is tottering on the edge! Will you wake up and save yourselves or will you once more be swept away by the flood?

Foreword

"I wish to tell the world what is theirs for the asking.

To try and give them a new viewpoint—in place of their erroneous ideas.

Before, I wrote what the Self saw only—now it is what *I know*."

My Tussle with the Devil

My Tussle with the Devil

IT was the hour when souls simply cling to their bodies by the merest thread—when I met His Satanic Majesty.

He is well named, for he is majestic in every sense of the word—majestic of mien—majestic of gesture, of expression, and a god to look upon.

He is a deceptive person, for one meeting him casually would think he was one of the great and good men of the day—abroad on errands of mercy and with kindness in his heart for all humanity. So carefully does he conceal his identity that he resembles most of mankind—who are one person to themselves and quite another to the world of men.

We met. He knew me, but I had not yet had the pleasure of knowing this majestic lord—or thought I had not—and so was flattered when he accosted me and made me welcome.

"I was told you were coming, and so came to meet you," he said, with a smile of geniality. "We hoped to have greeted you earlier."

"Just a minute," I said. "Who are you? Who told you I was coming?"

Making a sweeping gesture, and ignoring my questions, he continued:

"Our land is fair—as you see—but there are many wonders which I desire to show you. Wonders which are unheard of—not even dreamt of —and which will make you desire to remain among us, I feel confident."

With this, my arm was taken in friendly fashion, and we proceeded up an avenue lined with trees perfect in form and foliage—passed handsome houses, with playing fountains, flowers, and birds in abundance.

With a magnificent gesture he

swept all this out of the way. "The homes of our servants. We enter now the domains of those who rule and where we hope you will abide."

The turn of the street brought us to an estate situated on the crest of a magnificent mountain. Winding roads of dazzling whiteness and smoothness led through a garden of flowers and wonderful trees. Running streams made music, and the song of birds—with brilliant plumage.

With no word spoken—but many implied by gesture and nod—we reached at last the mansion. Transparent—the walls seemed—heavy the air, with perfume. It was a palace of dreams—resting in the hollow of my hand.

With a smile of winning sweetness he said:

"This is yours. Will you rest?"

"Mine! For what?" I exclaimed.

"Do you give palaces like this to all your visitors?"

"Not to all," he answered; "only to our favored ones."

"Why am I so favored, then? What have I done to bring me this?"

"Nothing," he answered, *"as yet,* but we have hopes of great things from you. We expect you will be of great benefit to us; will aid us in promoting our cause."

"And how?" I queried.

"Come, let us sit and sup and we will talk it over."

Leading me gently forward, we entered a banqueting hall, where costly viands and sparkling wines reposed among flowers; and gold and silver, and ruby and diamond, sapphire and emerald decked each goblet—while behind our places were fair women, who smiled and breathed perfume upon the air.

Too dazed to remonstrate, I took

my place, and, unconscious of what I did, sipped my wine from its jeweled goblet.

Lifting his wine, he said: "To our better acquaintance—our Brotherhood, I hope."

"To our better acquaintance, certainly—but what do you mean by Brotherhood?"

"That I will explain. In this mountain fastness there is a secret abode, which only the elect can enter, and where the members set in motion great events and accomplish great deeds. We have need of one like you to assist us."

"What do you feel I can do?" I asked. "My talents are slight. I do not comprehend my selection."

"Ah! That is not to be wondered at—for you have not correctly gauged your talents and ability.

"Do you realize that you have the greatest talent ever known—in one direction?"

"What!" I gasped.

"Quite true! I will tell you.

"In the beginning you were pre-
sented, by lesser gods, with a talent
for love of everything, with love for
the pure, for the true, for the beautiful. You aspired to be one of the
unknown workers for humanity—to
create beauty, in poem and song; to
weave for them music which would
make life an ecstacy.

To scatter happiness was your
ambition. Jealousy was unknown to
you, and envy a word you never even
thought of.

Kindness was your pass-word in
the realm from which you came—but
we, who were observing you, recognized a power much greater than you
knew—a power to work results magical in their effect—and so we came
near you and sought to make your
better acquaintance.

You were a shy bird, difficult to

catch, however, and it took us many eons of time before we finally won your confidence."

"What was this great ability?" I interrupted.

"You wish to know? That is well, for I see we shall be able to work more harmoniously if your interest is aroused," he replied. "I will tell you. It was—but why should I say 'it was,' rather, it is still, the great gift you possess, and which we desire to have you give to us in all its fullness. Let us review a bit what use you made of it.

First, you were disappointed in the love of the woman whom you desired, and so began its development— until love for man or woman had no place in your heart.

Then commenced your clear vision, which showed you the evil which was in all minds and hearts, and you recognized no one could be

trusted. Ultimately, you nearly per-
fected that branch of your gift, and
so had an honored seat at our coun-
cil table—and we desire you again to
take your place at its head."

"But why?" I interrupted, "did I
lose that exalted seat?"

"Alas!" he answered, "you went
back to your old habits. An animal
was the cause of your downfall—a
mongrel cur!"

"You interest me," I said. "Explain how that occurred."

"You were in a forsaken village—
having lost your way and wandered
there—and without food. Little by
little your strength left you, and you
lay down under a tree, with all hope
abandoned. A rustle in the dead
grass aroused you, and presently a
tiny, mangy dog crept up and licked
your hand.

The relief from the loneliness was
so great that you foolishly took the
cur in your arms."

"Foolishly!" I exclaimed.

"Yes, foolishly; for that was the beginning of your loss of power. True, the animal led you out to safety and warmth, eventually. But *what* a seed was sown!

Where before the harvest was well-nigh perfect, it now had the weeds of Pity and Gratitude—— *So* do the mighty fall!

That was a fatal sowing and reaping for you, for it even affected your view of men. You commenced to see in them bits of character before unseen. Such useless things as Consideration, Love and Pity!

Your habits, too, were affected by this poisonous weed. Where before you had been perfect in all ways vile, you now commenced to give up some of the most brilliant jewels—betrayal of women—the excitement and joy of perfect and exhilarating wines. Why! you even went so low as to prefer sparkling waters from Nature's sources."

Holding my jeweled goblet high, I laughed and said: "To what depths can man sink!"

"Ah! I rejoice to see you agree with me. It is well! We shall succeed together admirably, I feel sure," he made answer.

Then, drawing closer to me, "Now to our desires and agreement."

"By all means," I replied. "I am eager to hear your plan. For, certainly, if this domain is part of the reward, it interests me."

"Good! That is better," he replied.

"When you first left our abode and joined with others, who had contrary beliefs, we felt it was final—but as we watched and studied your soul— for you know, of course, souls are clearly visible to us—and saw there was within it, still, the desire to continue as one of us, I was given the task of keeping alive that seed, and adding to its force, so that in time a bountiful harvest might repay us.

We feel that time has arrived.

As I told you, this palace, with all it contains, its vault of priceless gems —such as are on your goblet, these fair women, and hundreds like them, are yours. Any honor you feel you desire shall be granted, and you shall be the lord of whatsoever you desire to possess."

At this I glanced around the hall. Looked at the smiling faces—slender, voluptuous forms—at the sparkling gems—at the vista which was spread before me through the open windows —and then I mused upon what I could possess in addition—all honors whatsoever I desired. Coming back, finally, to a study of His Majesty's face, I found his eyes fixed upon me.

"Will you accept?" he asked.

"That is a little mystery, too, of yours, is it not? You ask if I will accept all that counts in the world, but you have not yet told me what I am to do for it all. Tell me that side of the mystery," I replied.

"Only a simple thing!

Renew your association with us and take the leadership of the band which is ready to go forth and sow broadcast the seeds which are so much craved by the world. The seeds of Hate, of Malice, of Licentiousness, of Cruelty.

Helps us to rid the world of gayety which is simple and wholesome. Help us to give them a greater excitement. Let us arouse the idea of hunting within their breasts—but children for game—not birds, which are only beautiful and give song, that would be tame sport!

Take the lead and aid us to sow Revenge broadcast."

"Is that all?" I queried.

"All for the present," he answered. "Later, new things can be brought to successful issue, if you desire. But that will satisfy our Brotherhood for the present."

"Let us drink to our unity," he said, raising high his glass and looking with flashing eyes into mine.

I rose to my feet, goblet high.

"To our Brotherhood!" I shouted; "May it be annihilated forever!"

The Contest

The Contest

Yucatan—Time: Midnight

IFE met Death in the room of Joe, who lay on a bed in the corner, with a pain-racked body.

Suspense as to the visitant made him almost unconscious, yet thoroughly cognizant. It was as if some part of his brain stopped, while the rest leaped away from the body—then, with a whirl which made him reel, leaped back again.

Gazing at him from a chair which stood in front of the fire was a softly clad woman. In her hands was myrtle and thyme, which made mysterious shadows upon the wall.

His humble room seemed decorated by a master hand. Each individual article took on a luster hitherto unknown.

With a movement, however, his eyes were brought back to the door, through which a figure slowly entered. It was radiant with a light which dazzled. Entering slowly, it stopped at the foot of his bed and said, in a voice sweeter than any music ever heard.

"I am Death! Will you come with me to a Summerland where there is only joy, and pain is unknown?"

"Death!" he gasped. "You, Death! But you do not look as I thought Death did! You are beautiful!"

"Yes," replied the figure, "I am the most beautiful of all, except one, but my gifts are more beautiful than *all*.

I bring surcease from trials, freedom from pain, shelter from all storms and peace.

I,—who am so much feared by mankind,—have only joy and happiness.

Make ready and come with me!

I promise you all you have ever longed for—sunshine, flowers and beauty."

Keeping his eyes riveted on the figure, Joe sat erect and said:

"How am I to know you are not fooling me? You don't look like Death. I don't believe you!"

The figure smiled.

"That is not unusual," it replied, "for men have a false idea of me. They think I am old and hideous and take from them all they hold dear.

They do not know I give them all they have earned and bring them the solace of retrieving all past errors.

I give them the opportunity of seeing how and why they failed.

I watch their silly strivings ˙for wealth, their many useless mansions, their hates and loves—which are only envy in fancy dress—knowing the time will come when they will be obliged to open the door to me.

Some welcome me, for they have built their mansion and know it only awaits their coming; that joy and happiness are theirs—love, free from all malice, and beauty in every form.

They welcome me, because they have built their home on rock and it stands with door open to receive them, and they are not afraid, but rejoice.

"Others, however, fear me and refuse to look at me, saying, 'You are ugly! Go away!' And they shut their ears and refuse to be comforted.

They are afraid, for they have no mansion to which to go, but are homeless and feel that they are outcasts. Why? Not because of me, but because they have forgotten to prepare their mansion and so are homeless and beggars. They cling to worn-out trumpery, keeping much more from them than they possess.

Give up this mansion of yours and come and follow me to new fields which are filled to overflowing."

Joe still stared, too much overcome to reply, when from the chair by the fire a figure arose.

It was clad in soft clinging garments, with a veil which hid the face, and the voice was deep and harsh, with an undertone of sadness.

"Wait! Not yet can he give you his answer. He must choose between us."

At this Joe turned his eyes toward the new speaker, and seemed to find once again the ability to speak.

"Who are you?" he asked.

"Life!" the figure replied. "Life! With all its dreams, its passions, its joys. Life! which has given you all your pain and misery. Life! which has snatched from you all your youth, your joy, and given you only disillusionment!

Life! which promised you happiness, health, wealth, fame!

Life! which dances and sings and has no need for tomorrow. Will you stay with me? See! I hold out to you healing herbs that will bring forgetfulness and give you power to go on and achieve what you desire.

See! I offer you fame!

You shall be able to sit above others,—to cast them forth, to spit upon them. You shall be lord of the cities. Fairest women shall smile and caress you; men shall sue you for recognition. Will you stay?"

Joe made a motion of assent.

There was a moment's stillness, then, with a laugh which froze his blood, Life said:

"Again I win, and your beauty and your gifts are spurned, Death! Again I win."

Death smiled and said: "I am content. Show him your face!"

At this command the figure began to unwind from the head the drapery which had enveloped it, and Joe, with staring eyes, looked into a hollow shell, a skeleton!

Sleeping

Sleeping

Gangs
In suits of gray
Worked upon the highway
In a Southern State.
Stones
Were their companions,
Coarse food
Their nourishment.

Cruelty
Met often with Greed
And Fear
Lived with Hatred,
When Love
Sought entrance
On a night
In June,
Trying
All the entrances
Unavailingly,
And tiring at last.

67

Kindness came
And whispering
In Love's ear
Said:
"Down the road
You will find open several houses.
Better go!
I will watch here."

Love
Gave thanks,
And with bounding steps
Went gayly to the Highway.
The sun
Was hot
And the stones were sharp,
But the time for rest was near,
And a little ripple
Was running along the highway,—
A tiny little wave
Of Joy.

Love
Seeing this,

Danced with glee
And began to sing:
"Come with me
Where the flowers bloom
And birds make music
All the noon.

Sunshine
Dances,
Girls give glances
To the moon.

Friends
Take chances,
Gay their fancies,
Come with me."

Startled
Glances went down the line,
And Love swept on
To the end,
Seeking
Entrance in each heart
And sending thrills

With delight,
Until
To each one
Passed the word
"Love is here!"

Backs
Grew straighter,
Faces brighter,
Down the line.

God
Crept nearer
Saying:
"Come with me!
Take
No chances
With the sleepers—
Come with me!"

And down
The highway
Swept the summons,
"Come with me!"

Gray garments
Changed
To gold,
And only
Hatred
And Fear
Were left uncalled
From their sleep.

Yearning

Yearning

HE lamps on the street throw fitful shadows upon the pavements, which glisten with many raindrops.

Walking slowly, with bent shoulders and bowed head, is a man with slightly graying hair. Round and round the square he walks, glancing neither to the right nor left, until finally, wearying, he crosses the street and enters a house where the curtains are closely drawn.

Bits of smilax, rose leaves and trodden violets can be seen about the steps, and as he opens the door, the air is charged with escaping perfume.

With a hasty glance at the heavy draperies which conceal the opening to *the* room, he mounts hurriedly the stairs, and with trembling hands turns the knob of a door.

75

Gently he pushes it wide, and the soft gleam of the lamp plays upon the silken draperies of a woman's room.

No sound breaks the stillness as the man closes the door and with a heart-broken cry throws himself upon his knees by the bedside.

His frame shakes from head to foot as his arms are thrown across the bed which had so recently held all his world.

At last, worn out by the battle, his body relaxes, and released from its leash, the spirit meets the occupant of the room.

Clasped in his arms, with gentle, loving fingers she strokes his face and says:

"I am still here with you—always, as you are now with me."

His clasp tightens as he sobs:

"I thought that you were dead—that you had left me."

"Loving you, how could I leave you?" she answered. "And there is no such thing as death! One only changes!

I am just as you are now; and as we have been each night we have gone out together. The only change is that during a few hours you go back to the world of business, while I wait for you in the land of art

Dry your eyes, beloved, for when you weep, you keep me from creating the beautiful things we have longed for. All the material is here at my hand, but I must be free to work.

The clocks of the city are striking the hour for you to begin your work and for me also. Go now! And tonight we will tell each other of what we have accomplished."

The striking of the hour breaks the stillness of the room, and the man by the bedside stirs and then gazes with unseeing eyes at the empty bed and the room with its softly glowing lamp.

A well-remembered perfume floats upon the air and his hair is brushed as by a fairy wind.

With arms outstretched, he rises to his feet.

"Tell me it is true! That, if it was a dream, that dreams are the truth of life! Give me some sign that I may know, my darling. I must know! I must! Give me some little sign!"

As he gazes at the curtain which conceals the doorway, there is a faint rustle of silken drapery, and a shadow seems upon it for just a moment.

The lamp burns low, the man sits motionless.

"Was it true? Was it a sign, or was it only a movement by the wind?"

II.

Seated on the sidewalk, crying bitterly, is a small boy, holding in his arms a dog.

The grief of the child attracts a passer-by, who questions:

"What is the trouble, little man?"

Between sobs, the child explains that he missed his pet and found it in the road.

"He didn't come when I called. He always minds. And now he doesn't tell me anything! Why doesn't he?"

"Let me see, little man," says the stranger, and stoops to take the dog, which the boy clasps more tightly.

Putting his hand on the child's head: "Poor little man! I am soꞁry, but your little friend will never do any of those things again, for he is dead."

With a cry of joy the child jumps up, and says:

"Is that it? Well, that's all right; for now he will always stay where I am."

With a quick gesture the man put out his hand and caught the child.

"What do you mean by that? Why are you happy, now, when I tell you he is dead?"

Gazing upward at the man's face, the child answers:

"Why! Mother told me so. She says there is no death—there only is another life—and when we love any one very much they never leave us.

She says that when its daylight we cannot see them because they are so beautiful, but that at night we can, when we go to sleep—and that's our real life—when we think we are only sleeping."

The man clutched at the child almost wildly.

"You believe that, little man?"

"Of course! It's true! Now, I must take Fido to mother, for she knows what to do to make him beautiful—and then tonight we'll play hide-and-seek, as we were going to this morning."

With a happy and joyous "good-bye" ringing in his ears, the man gazed at the little figure flying down the street.

"I wonder! Yes! It was a sign, for is it not said—'A little child shall lead them!' "

Animals

My wish is to widen the horizon. It is important for humanity to *know*. It must recognize the oneness of everything.

We will write of more than man.

I will give a series: First—Beasts; then, Flowers and Jewels.

Weariness

I.—THE KING

PACING forward — backward — backward — forward, to and fro—a King.

With world weary eyes he gazes out of his window in search of his soul's desire.

Before him a seething mass of heads, with eyes riveted upon him. Immovable, he stands and contemplates them.

Of what do they think?

Have they souls which long and cry out, day and night, for liberty?

Or are they satisfied with the narrow ring in which they move?

Do they know the joy of freedom: of vast expanses?

A surge of hatred passes through him and he has a longing to slay that sodden mass. Then it passes, and with a weary movement once more he paces to and fro.

Of what does *he* think?

Does he know that once again has been enacted an old drama and a King sold into captivity, or does he feel that it should be said:

"Forgive them, for they know not what they do."

II. THE TOILER

Up — down — down — up—from early morn.

Up—down—with slow and steady strides, until the rich brown earth holds up eager hands to receive its gifts.

Up—down — down—up—wearily plods the Toiler until the sun is high, when, with a long-drawn sigh, the time of rest is welcomed.

A bit of shade, a refreshing drink,

and a little rest before the weary round begins again.

Up — down — down—up—day in and out.

" 'Monotonous,' you say? Yes! if only the thought of the weary rounds is held. Compensation comes from a pat on the neck, which tells of appreciation and affection and the knowledge of being a necessary part of the whole. The harvest *I* sow is reaped and lessens in other lands the harvest of the Reaper.

"Up — down — down — up, with a stronger pull, for I am doing my bit, and

" 'To him who is faithful in small things much shall be given.' "

The Slave

I.

EAR the door sits an impressive looking man.

"It is growing dark, mademoiselle; just turn up the light."

The interior is flooded with light at this command.

In a far corner lies a spaniel, gazing with pain-stricken eyes at the man. He is too worn in spirit to do more than give a feeble move, now and then, to first one ear and then another. But worn and spent as he is, his eyes are alert for movement on the part of the man, and as the man rises from his chair, the dog utters a faint cry of fear and begins to shake; but his trembling gradually ceases as the man goes in the opposite direction, and he closes his eyes in complete weariness.

Each moment has seemed hours to him, for fear has dragged at his soul.

What new torture awaited him when that huge form moved—to what unknown horror was he to be compelled to submit?

Helpless—chained—and too weak to fight, he was at the mercy of THAT, which sat in front of him.

It looked like his beloved master in form, but the voice was different and the touch——

At the thought of the hand which had caressed him only two days, or was it two years ago, he gave a little whimper, which was quickly stifled as he recalled that the slightest move on his part brought that which gave him only misery—pulling, testing, delicate nerves pressed, and pain indescribable.

Silence reigns, and at last, worn out, he closes his eyes and sleeps.

Once more he is in a room where

sparkles a glowing fire, and, with ears alert, listens for a well-known step. Joy permeates him as it comes nearer and nearer, and then the door opens.

With a waving of banner and joyous greeting he leaps to meet a caress and welcome:

"Well, old boy! Glad to see me? Bring me my slippers. There's a good fellow."

The joy of taking some part of that dear one close to him and carrying it where he knew it belonged! The excitement of returning and hearing "Right you are, old boy! now the other," and then the delicious sense of work well done and the praise earned, and the happiness and joy of the hand on his head, while both relaxed to the warmth of the fire.

A sudden pang of pain rouses him, and the remembrance is shattered and dismay takes its place.

What has happened? All he can recall is standing on the doorstep, waiting for that promised walk, and suddenly a jerk, and he is flying through the air and is thrust into a black and yelling mass of his brothers.

Then a brilliantly lighted place and a gruff voice, which says:

"That's the one. He's a thorough-bred. Bring him."

Running, darting this way, that way, snapping at his brothers who bar his escape, he dashes here, there, everywhere, looking in vain for an outlet, only to be cornered at last, with the same kind of a jerk which had torn him away from his door-step.

"Put up a fight, didn't he? The experiment will be all the more interesting now, for the nerves are excited."

Then, straps and buckles which

held him down, and cruel wires which prevented his breathing, and then THAT which was at the back of the room, standing over him with shining things, and then such pain as made him forget all things as he sank down—and down—and down!

With a start, he realizes there has been a movement in the room, and a shadow looms toward him. In vain to shrink—to avoid that hand which will soon be upon him, for he is chained and unable to move.

What new terror awaits him?

His heart beats to suffocation and his eyes seek dumbly for aid.

Nearer and nearer comes the shadow, and he abandons all hope, and with a cry of despair his body relaxes, as a figure looms over him.

Again the firelit room and a loved voice:

"Come, boy! Let's to bed and sleep."

With a mighty struggle he forces the spirit to rise. and once more opens his eyes, to find the fire light vanished and the loved voice silent—only a looming doom with shining things over him, and a voice, angry with thwarted ambition.

"Too late! He's dead."

But a spark of the spirit still lingers in the body, and the faithful eyes see a firelit room and a beloved form, and with a farewell wave of his banner, obeys the command:

"Let's sleep!"

FREEDOM

II.

Worn and weary, a man enters a room where a fire burns upon the hearth.

Throwing himself into a chair, he glances at the vacant rug at his feet, and, with a sob in his voice, says:

"Old Boy! No slippers for me to-night by my old faithful."

No sound breaks the stillness, and he gazes forelornly towards his room.

Then he sits erect—rigid, for through the door comes a dearly loved figure, head high and banner waving in anticipation of "Well done, good and faithful servant," and love shining in his eyes, and in his mouth—a slipper!

With suspended breath the man watches, and even at the touch of cold nose upon his hand, remains rigid. Then, with a cry, he throws

out his arms to encircle his comrade—
only empty air greets him.

But at his feet lies—a slipper!

In stupefaction he looks at it, and
then around the room.

Nothing!

Nothing? No! surely something is
still in the familiar place—something
which is faithful always and remains
where love keeps the place!

A light of understanding breaks
over the man's face as he takes the
slipper.

"Oh! ye of little faith!"

Flowers

Missionaries

I.

UST outside of a walled city there is a field of white—little, delicate, slim emissaries of peace, wafting their messages of healing broadcast. With a ringing of delicate musical bells, they say:

"Come with me! Here is joy and peace."

Within the walls a lonely watcher in a tower looks and listens.

Hidden from view are the tools of trade.

Gazing on the field, he muses on the infallibility of the law, which with undeviating regularity brings forth the thousands of tiny Heralds. Surely they are a symbol of some part of that Great Whole—some plan is back of their being!

He looks over the walled city which, he guards, and nowhere is there anything which is as wonderful as what lies outside.

Ah! now he knows!

Outside is Freedom—with all its loveliness and fragrance.

Outside is God's World with only bells, orchestra of rustling leaves and the waving baton of the trees.

Outside all is Peace—Harmony.

And what is within —— ——?

Envy, Vice, Hatred, and stalking ever at the head Fear—as Leader— whose orchestra is made up of glittering instruments of torture, deafening batteries, and with Triumph as the theme.

With gold, jewels and honors he lures to his band all within the walls, murmuring:

"My lands shall include all things. Nothing shall exist which is as perfect as my Empire."

But——

Outside—are dainty, delicate, slim bits of loveliness, which, with gentle nods and soft waves of perfume bring the message that, Outside, all is as God intended, for——

"Consider the lilies! They toil not, neither do they spin, and yet I say unto you that Solomon in all his glory was not arrayed like one of these."

Jewels

Multitudes

ITHIN the darkest recesses there is a vast multitude seeking expression — rising with each multitude a little higher.

Rubies, who gather to themselves the fading glory of the sun, secretly desire the millions of rays which the diamond has secured,—while Sapphires, holding the blue winged lights of the moon,—seek in vain to acquire the rustling of trees and grasses, the running of water,—within their form.

Insensate?

Round and round the spiral they travel,—ever spurred, by the force lying within each and every one, to be more than they are and to express All!

* * * * *

I recall my youth, in fancy, as so many jewels tied to dark recesses while aspiring;—The desire to voice the Rubies of Multitudes, in Dislike and Hatred—reveling in the Emeralds of wealth, and desire for honors —while ever knocking at my door was the Sapphire, laden with gifts of Aspiration.

In vain the Diamond beckoned,— in vain sought to convince me that within *that* recess was all I desired— that *there* was to be found, mingled together All as One.

* * * * *

The Multitudes hurry past, unconscious that in their path lies the Diamond. Hurrying, scurrying, they push and jostle in a vain endeavor to amass Rubies, Emeralds and Sapphires. little realizing that in their

own door yard lies the most priceless
jewel of all:

The Diamond of Love.

I was of the Multitude:—

Reason said:

"Seek Emeralds.   What matter if
you borrow Rubies of Hatred to
gain! Seek Emeralds!"

Mind said:

"What are Emeralds? It is Sapphires you desire. Sapphires—which
lead you by a radiant path to the sky
—to starry realms—to lands where
Inspiration dwells.

"Seek!

"Seek Sapphires!"

Spirit said:

"You are wrong. It is none of
these you desire. Seek the Diamond.
Search for it high and low. Do not
be beguiled by colors which lure.
Seek the purest of all.

"Seek!

"Search for Diamonds!"

Alas! the colors of the rainbow caught me and I bathed in its rays.

Now I go seeking! Seeking everywhere—Diamonds—only Diamonds.

Remembrances

Remembrances

I.

THE SENTINELS:

Uniforms of green—hardy and erect, they wait until mustered—keeping watch throughout the seasons.

* * * * *

THE ARMY:

In glittering array the army stands for inspection.

Russet, gold and green are their uniforms, with trimmings of scarlet.

Unmoved they will stand and receive all onslaughts—and if some fall in the battle, those remaining will still be firm of purpose—turning ever a smile of welcome and holding out arms to those who seek them.

Red and russet and gold——

Green and bronze and scarlet——

How brave in all their glory—how steadfast to their purpose—how gratefully do they bend their heads when a wave of love goes to them!

Majestic—serene—content to fill their allotted place—asking not the perfume of lilies, nor scent of roses—seeking not the sparkling splendor of jewels—content with the Emerald, Ruby and Topaz, which they hold within their own domain.

So muses the recruit, as with head high and shoulders back he wanders through the woods—saying farewell to all the friends of his boyhood.

The Sentinels!

How they have guarded the old home from the blasts!

`How joyfully have the regiment given of their life, in order that others might revel in their force, and uniting to protect all who sought their shelter. This was what he must keep ever in mind—to follow his army

friends and do with gladness whatever came his way—without thought
of honors—only with love for all—
and cheerfully obey.

Taking a bit of the uniform of his
sentinel friends, and a bit of russet
and gold and scarlet, too, he softly
places them in his pocket and with a
salute goes out to join his company.

Munitions

Munitions

Hardware Store—Time: Midday

Gazing out of a window which overlooked a training field for soldiers was a grizzled old man. Time had left his impress with no gentle mark, yet around the eyes was a lingering spark of youth, and about the mouth the lines told of a gentle and loving spirit.

As his eyes roamed over the field a small squad came into view, marching in "twos" and wheeling into "fours" and "right about," as the command was given.

The gaze of the man grew more intense, and the lines about the mouth deepened, while, slowly, a flush of pride, which could not be controlled, swept over the face, and unconsciously his shoulders squared and his back straightened as his son came into view.

The straight boyish figure marched and wheeled in perfect unison with his comrades, but there was an indefinable power in the set of his head and poise of the body, which bespoke determination and control beyond the ordinary.

Suddenly the silence is broken by a voice, and the man, with a start, turns from the window and faces a customer who has entered so quietly that even the bell on the door has failed to make any sound.

"Good-day to you, sir," said the customer. "I have been searching the town for some munitions. Have you any?"

"A complete stock—of everything," the old man answered.

"Well, I want both large and small. Something suitable for a double-barrel and a self-repeater. Can you supply me?"

"Yes. How much of each will you have?"

The man hesitated, and then putting his hand in his pocket, he drew out a bundle of notes and handful of gold.

"That is all I have. Wrap up all you can give me for that amount."

The old man gazed at the money and then his eyes traveled toward the field where young boys eagerly answered to the commands sent forth: Forward! March!

Turning to his shelves, he took down, first, a box marked "For double-barrel," and wrapped it up. Then, next, came a box labelled "self-repeater—all sizes," and then, with great care, came the last—"deadly mixture—guaranteed."

Each one he made into a separate package and then pushed them toward his visitor, who thanked him and departed.

Gathering up the gold and bank notes, the old man went to a safe in the far corner, and, opening the door, took out a drawer marked "Munition Fund" and put the money into it, smiling as he did so.

Taking his place again at the window, he gazed over the field, lost in thought, and reviewing in memory the years of his youth, when he, too, obeyed the command "Forward! March!"

A sound made him turn, and he was confronted by his customer, who, in a state of extreme anger, waved his packages at him, exclaiming:

"I asked for munitions! See what you have given me!"

The old man came forward, and taking the boxes, proceeded to read:

"For double-barrel—warranted, 'Kindness!'

"For self-repeater—guaranteed, 'Joy!'

"Deadly mixture—Love!

"Well, my friend, what is wrong? This is all as it should be!"

"Should be? I wanted gunpowder and cartridges—not that stuff!"

"You have lost your way, my man. On this planet those are our only munitions."

Going Home

Going Home

HE sky was heavy with menacing clouds, and wind —howling dismally as it blew through the trees— when I met a wayfarer who was walking, with downcast eyes, along the highway which skirted the town.

Gazing at him sharply, I met a furtive glance, which held within it pleading, and yet had an assurance which was compelling. He hesitated when we came abreast, and as I felt in the mood for converse, I bade him "Good-evening."

"It is a *good* evening, is it not," he replied. "Good, in its freedom of elements. They make merry to-night."

This was a strange answer, and my curiosity was piqued, and I felt constrained to lead him on further.

"You feel the elements are enjoying themselves?" I asked.

"Thoroughly," he answered, "but one never knows what their decision will be."

"Decision! What do you mean?"

"Whether they will be content with a simple little frolic or if they have mischief in their minds," he answered.

"Mischief! in their minds!" Surely that is a strange expression to use regarding the wind and clouds."

"Strange? You, too, find it strange?"

As he spoke he looked at, and yet again, not at me, but through me, and then continued:

"To me there is nothing in all the Universe without mind. All is alive and all make merry or are sad—bring joy or sorrow, as their bent may be. Just as man can be kind, or cruel, make beautiful the world or destroy, so do the Beings dwelling in the elements.

Tonight they will tell me whether I make merry or pass out in sorrow."

"That is a strange thing you say! 'Make merry or pass out in sorrow.' What does that portend?" I questioned.

"Sir," he answered, "you do not understand, and yet you look to me as one of us.

Tonight I am going home and I have not yet made the necessary decision as to my going—whether it shall be a right merry leave-taking or one of sadness. Today a winged messenger came and told me my exile was ended and I could start for my home tonight."

"And where is your home?" I asked.

"That is for me to decide."

"For you to decide! Is it not where you lived last?" I asked.

"Alas! no. I have lost that beautiful place, but there are others for me to choose from. Or, perhaps, I shall elect to remain here a little longer—I have left so much undone. I find so many words unspoken which would have given joy, perhaps, —so many things postponed. I did not give heed to the passing of hours for I felt years were before me. But the summons has come and I am to go home—to go to the house I have been building."

His eyes were fixed on the horizon and my gaze followed him, for so intent was he that I felt there was something there I could see. Then, suddenly, the wind swept past us with a mighty gust. The trees bent beneath its force, and. with a sudden upflinging of his head he turned toward me, and said, pointing to the horizon:

"See! There is my road and just at the end of the lane my home. Yes!

after all, it will be good to go back.
The weeds are in the garden and it
seems neglected, for no love has entered into the care of it; but there
are blossoms among the grass which
has overgrown the doorstep, and I
can make it beautiful, after all. Just
a little care, a bit of love, and time
spent in taking out the nettles, and—
yes, it can be made a home. See!
there are children down the street. I
can build swings and make toys for
their playthings, and it can be a merry
place."

Watching him with amazement, I
moved along at his side, speaking no
word, until we came to a little shanty
all by itself, on the dreariest part of
the bluff. It was forbidding, and I
remembered it was the place of the
old miser and renegade of the town.
As we reached the door a sudden
noise within made me pause, and I

pushed open the rickety door. From a corner of the hut came a voice:

"So you have come at last! I have just been waiting until you reached me, for I am going home. Going home to just a little place like this, but it has flowers in its yard and there are children who need me."

There came a sudden terrific whirl of wind and dust—the door slammed to and my knees shook,—for I was alone—no soul in sight, no habitation—only scurrying clouds and trees bending under the blast, while above me floated down a voice:

"I am going home! Are you ready? Make ready! for soon you, too, will be

GOING HOME

My Hearth

My Hearth

RANDFATHER sits in an old armchair. The back of it boasts an anti-macassar in many colors, while the seat has a patchwork cushion.

Grandmother occupies a low rocker, which moves slowly to and fro, as she softly hums the hymn of the Sunday service.

Keeping silence is grandfather's "long suit"—while making, in reality, *my* life.

He is a sturdy old chap, with a will and determination which has carried him beyond anti-macassars and patchwork cushions, and centered itself upon me   No fly was ever more helpless!

I make the announcement:

"Life is going to give me something more than this country town."

Silence reigns on the left of the hearth, and creak! creak! and a gentle hum answers me from the right.

Minutes, which seem hours, pass—but emboldened by the pictures seen in the coals, once more a voice is heard:

"When I am grown up I am going to the city! and I am going to travel! and I am going around the world! and I am going to make a *heap* of money and be famous!"

Silence!

Creak—creak!!

Half of eternity passes—when once more, emboldened spirit takes hold of courage and dares to speak.

"I have made up my mind and I am going to do what I said, and *nothing* shall keep me from it!"

Silence!

Creak—creak!!

Years pass in review. The coals burn to ash, and from a far-off sphere issues a voice:

"I'll have none of that nonsense. You'll do what you are told to do!"

Silence!

Creak—creak!!

The pictures fade. A clock strikes. The chair groans and grandfather goes in search of his lantern.

Creak—creak! and then the touch of a gentle hand and a voice made sweet from singing many hymns:

"Make your pictures, my boy, for they will come true. Make them, hold them, and most of all *believe* in them. Good night."

Silence!

Creak—creak!!

The Three H's

The Three H's

FOREWORD

Without Health, Life seems Hell.
With Harmony it becomes Heaven.
And when combined, Happiness,
here, is the result.

The Three H's

PART I.

I N a tavern, which was on the waterfront and visited mostly by sailors on shore leave, lay a semblance of a man. He was tattered and in rags. Crouching at his feet was a dog as forlorn as he was and in a starved condition.

Standing around the pair was a circle of men—the regular habitués of the place.

"Where'd you find him, Pete?" inquired a sour-visaged standee.

"On the wharf. I heard the dog, and as my boy wants a cur, I followed the sound. But love ye! I couldn't touch the dog, for he was that crazy at seeing me. Seemed like he would never stop running around me—but always out of reach—first to me and then to the bundle.

Finally I got Steve there, and together we set to work to pick him up, and do you know, that cur jest settled down as quiet and followed at our heels. Seemed as if that was what he wanted."

Here the men looked sheepishly at each other, as if each was ashamed at the emotion which stirred within him and was afraid lest it be observed.

Finally the first speaker took courage and said:

"Well, come on, let's see what's wrong. Get some brandy—and, oh! hell! give the dog something to drink and eat, too."

In a moment there was action, where before there was inertia. One bringing a basin of warm water and a towel, another brandy, while the rest undertook to look after the dog, who refused to move away from the man's side, however, and refused even the food and drink offered until he saw that aid was being given to his companion. Then, with a growl of satisfaction, which contained as well a despairing moan—as if the relief of nourishment was almost too great to bear—he commenced to devour ravenously what was placed before him, and gave thanks, in all directions, with a waving and vigorous tail message.

Just as he made his final thump of gratitude, the figure of his companion stirred and moaned, and instantly the dog was over the heads of the men, bending over his master and wildly lapping his face and hands, from which the dirt and blood had been removed.

It was a face of refinement, delicate in its outline, and with an expression which held the crowd silent.

Whether the brandy, which had been forced down his throat, or the caressing of the dog aroused him, it is difficult to say—for it was to the dog he turned his eyes, not to the men standing about him, and as his hand touched the animal it gave a wild yelp of gladness.

At this, a glimmer of a smile passed over the face—a smile tender as a mother's and filled with the love and adoration of a child.

"Dakta, dear old Dakta," he murmured feebly.

At the sound of his voice the dog laid down and moaned from very joy.

The man caressed the animal with the gentleness of a woman until it subsided and rested in peace against his body.

Then his eyes wandered over the group, which had stood silent and awe-struck at the emotion of the dog. With a smile which radiated over them all, he said:

"So you are Dakta's good friends. I welcome you, comrades."

A shuffling of feet answered him, and glances shot from right to left, but before any one had summoned the courage to reply, he continued:

"It seems strange to you, I perceive, for me to welcome you as Dakta's friends. Men live all their lives with the most precious of jewels at their door and are unaware of it. Often it is wrapped in poor covering and often, too, in gorgeous raiment. I was one of those men."

Here he stopped and stroked the dog, who now lay quiet and content, glancing up, now and then, into his friend's face.

After a moment of silence, the man raised himself and looked intently into each face.

A furtive smile answered his query, on some faces, while others looked away, and yet, without their volition, their eyes came back and rested on his face.

"Come nearer, comrades. Sit at ease while I tell you of this jewel, which you all have within your reach and which Dakta, too, possesses."

The men seated themselves quietly —one might almost say, reverently— so different was their attitude from their usual manner.

When the men were settled, his glance traveled over them all.

"Do you know that you have here untold riches?"

"To hell, we have!" ejaculated Steve.

"Exactly," responded the stranger. "That is just it—Hell!—and that is paved with untold wealth—good intentions."

"Huh!" snorted one of the listeners, "much good that wealth does a feller; you can't buy a drink with that."

"You are mistaken, my friend. It does you the greatest good in the world, and I will prove it to you; and, furthermore, it will purchase for you all the drinks you desire. Will you hear?"

"Fire away."

II.

"When I was a lad, I was puny, sickly, and in consequence was barred from the joy of companions and play.

My parents were too occupied with their great responsibilities—my father amassing wealth and my mother keeping her place as the leader of society—to give any special attention to the offspring who only upset the routine of the household by illness at inopportune times, and so the care was relegated to hirelings—who were paid for their time and gave accordingly only the efforts of their hands, with no thought that they possessed a heart.

I was kept out of doors constantly, and my only companion was the mother of Dakta. We grew up together, and it was the exercise given me from very joy and ecstacy—together with the love and devotion, which I felt for the first time, and realized did exist—which restored me gradually to health.

Next I became acquainted with selfishness and cruelty, for my playmate—having added to the joy of the world, five beautiful downy bits of life—was taken away from me, for she brought a good price with four of her children. Money was of more importance than love. Dakta, here, was left behind, however, for the stableman, for he had looked after her mother.

It was from the stableman that I received my first lesson as to the wealth which was to be obtained.

He was an ugly, brutal looking

man, dirty and unkempt most of the time, but to me he was a very god, for each day he came to the wicket of the fence, with Dakta in his arms, and with a smile which was like a beam of sunshine, he would say, "Hey! little master, here she is," and with that he would put Dakta through the wicket.

Each day ever since she has been with me, sharing joy and sorrow and teaching me with infinite patience and love the great lessons of life— Faithfulness, Gratitude, Cleanliness, Godliness and Work.

For ten years she has been steadfast and her love unchanged, although I have led her through the mire many times, and hunger and cold have been her portions."

Here he put his hand upon the dog and turned its face upward, and, looking into its eyes, said:

"But never lack of love, old girl! Never that!"

The dog kept its eyes upon him as he spoke, and the men were silent as it gave a little whimpering answer and licked the man's hand.

Turning once more to his circle of listeners, the man continued his story:

"I have called you Dakta's comrades for she selected you, and her judgment is unerring in regard to those who have wealth."

Here he smiled, and in a whimsical tone said:

"She is an aristocrat, and traces her family many generations, and therefore shuns those who do not belong to her class. For we have mingled with each and every class—having been the invited guests of multimillionaires, pampered social leaders, and sat at the table of all of the rulers of the world. We have dwelt in hovels, slept in the desert, and wandered forsaken and alone along the highways.

Tonight our pilgrimage ends, for we have won the fight and I am once more in possession of my soul."

The music of his voice had stilled all the warring elements within each man, and they scarcely breathed for fear of losing that which they felt had entered and warmed them. There was no need for the gin and whisky, which had kept the blood heated, for there was a glow from the eyes of both man and dog which made them warmer than they had ever been.

Putting his hand on the dog's head, he said.

"Attention. Dakta! It is time to choose."

Immediately the dog was on its haunches, ears erect, nose quivering and eyes going from man to man.

"I have called you Dakta's comrades, but you are mine as well—for 'Lo! the stranger was at your gates and you took him in and bathed and fed him.'

We need helpers, and Dakta shall choose. After she has selected each one for his particular office, we will discuss the work to be done. I will tell you in advance, however, that you will receive greater payment for your services than you have ever had before."

The men were as graven images.

Then came the command:

"Leader! Dakta!"

With a dignity which was inspiring, Dakta walked around each man, looking, first, intently into each face and then sniffing. Having made the rounds, she walked to the most besotted looking, and putting her paws on his knee, looked up into his face and whined, meanwhile waving in triumph the flag of her tail.

The man at whose knee she stood put out a trembling and hesitating hand, whereupon Dakta gave a little yelp of pleasure, and kissed it.

At this the entire attitude of the man changed, and he sat erect, where before his body had slouched, and his head went up until the carriage of the body was that of a ruler, and he arose from his chair and, with eyes alight, followed Dakta to the right hand of the man and seated himself on the floor beside him.

Again came the command:

"Treasurer! Dakta!"

Once more the dog made its rounds, stopping finally in front of a man who had kept his eyes upon the ground. He stirred uneasily at the touch of Dakta's paws upon his knee, and made a movement as if he would push her away. At that she gave a little cry and jumped into the lap of the man and commenced to lick his face.

The man made no move for a moment, and then suddenly clasped her in both arms and hid his face in her neck.

"Well chosen, Dakta!" said her master.

"Come, comrade, and sit at my left."

The man rose, still holding Dakta close to his heart, but his head raised high and his eyes straight ahead—and took his place at the left, upon the floor.

Again came the command:

"The Mender! Dakta!"

Wriggling out of the arms of the man who held her, she once more made her rounds, this time stopping before Steve. and whining as if in recognition.

Steve looked down into the animal's face and said:

"Hell! What *are* you?"

At this Dakta leaped about him in ecstacy and tugged at his coat, until Steve put out his brawny hand and caressed her head.

Once again came the voice of her master:

"Well selected. Let him sit in front of me, Dakta."

And dragging Steve by the coat, she brought him in front of her master, who put out his hand and said:

"Welcome, Brother."

As the man's hand touched his, a smile went over the face of Steve and glorified it, and he silently took his place as indicated.

Once more rang out a command:

"The Light Bearer! Bring the Light Bearer, Dakta."

This time Dakta made a flying leap into the lap of Pete, and dog and man gazed into each other's eyes. Then, as Dakta sprang to the floor, Pete followed her where she led him, to her master, who held out both hands and said:

"My Brother!" And Pete passed around and placed his back next to that of the man.

A final command rang out:

"Select the brothers of each!" And Dakta made her rounds, bringing two to sit next to the Treasurer, two next to the Leader, two next to the Mender, and two next to the Light Bearer, coming herself to curl up at her master's feet.

His eyes traveled over the men seated about him, now all with their heads erect and smiles upon their faces, and joy radiating from them all.

In a voice sweeter than any music, he said:

"Hell becomes Heaven when there is Harmony!

Is it not so, Brothers?"

The Senses

The Senses

SEEING:—

From my nest on shore I gaze across the sea to a tiny speck of white which appears on the horizon—a fluttering sail.

Suddenly, a swiftly darting thing of gray—a puff of smoke—

I strain my eyes in vain, but nowhere can be seen a fluttering sail of white or the darting thing of gray.

Only the ever-moving sea, gleaming with light!

———

FEELING:—

What tragedy has been enacted?

How many souls have silently bid adieu to the sunshine and the sea?

To what home is the news carried?

How many hearts are made to suffer?

How many homes bereft?

TASTING:—

I sit and gaze from my nest on land, but only a wall of gray can I distinguish.

Suddenly upon my lips a taste of salt!

Can it be that I, too, have been submerged and the waters of the sea caress my lips?

Alas! no! for the gray wall fades away and before my eyes is a sunlit sea with nothing in sight and upon my lips only my tears.

———

HEARING:—

From out my nest I gaze upon the sea. Gray it is, from leaden sky.

A deadly silence—then the tramp of myriad feet.

Suddenly the stillness is shattered by a volley and the last honors of the land are given to my all!!

TOUCHING:—

From outside my nest I gaze upon the sea.

My hands clasp only the leaves of many flowers and dampened earth, when leaden sky is reft and the tears of the angels of heaven fall upon my head in understanding,—and are added to the sea!

From out my nest I gaze across the sea.

A sunlit, sparkling sea
A gleaming dancing sea—
"All joy! all hope! be thine,"
It seems to say,
"For life has just begun."

Fancies

Fancies

Birds go seeking
Mates,
All on a day made gay.
   "Trees are blooming,
    Branches waiting,—
    Will you come?"
Shy the answer—
Swift surrender—
Roundelays are heard.

Time is flying,
Summer coming,
When the families
Say farewell.

In a pasture green
Fair flowers bloom;
Gay their faces—
Bright their dresses.

Swiftly seeking,
Whirling, wheeling,
Comes a flock
At noon.

"Here are daisies,
Sweetest grasses,
Buttercups and clover,
Let us linger, sip and treasure."

Summer passes,
Grasses perish,
But in sweetness
Is Springtime cherished.

Daylight passes,
Night approaches,
Lights begin to gleam.
In the houses
One can fancy
Nestlings tucked to rest.

———

Good night, sea,
Good night world,
All my soul goes out
To thee.
Happy meeting,
Friendly greeting
Upon the milky way.

TRUSTING

Upon the ocean wide
Two little ships set sail.

Over an ocean blue
Two little birds sailed true.

Kneeling upon a nursery floor
Two little children fair.

Under a star-lit sky
A youth and a maiden, shy.

With sightless eyes and folded hands,
Old age murmurs, "God knows best."

Faith—trust—love—courage!
That is all—God does the rest.

THOUGHTS

Thinking, thinking, thinking,
As the needle travels to and fro
Through sheerest linen—finest lace—
Weaving patterns—all unseen,
Upon its face.
Pictures vivid, pictures dim,
Pictures gay and with sadness grim.
Tiny feet—clinging hands—
All are in the fabric's sheen.

Unseen tracery takes its place,
To weave again its mystic theme.

THINKING

The only value of thinking
Is thinking of things worth while,
Of thinking of what you want to be,
And thinking of things to do
For the folks—who know not the
    value
Of thinking of things worth while.
All that you are, or will be,
Is vested in thinking,
And it's the thoughts worth while,
And the deeds well planned,
Which build your mansion here—and
    there,
So what are **you thinking now**—
    there?

Oh! the hours we spend,
And the days we spend,
In thinking no thoughts at all—
For the only thoughts— which really
     count—
Are the thoughts of love sent out to
     all,
For they are the thoughts worth
     while.

Yesterday—To-day

Yesterday—To-day

A Fantasy in Three Parts

PART I.—YESTERDAY

ITTLE wisps of clouds I meet as I wander by the sea,—fragile as lacy petticoats that imprison the form. Useless they seem to be, but as I watch I think I see a form. Multiplying, I mistake seeming for fact, and revel in the vision they recall.

Cloudless skies—dazzling sunshine —heavy scent of flowers, and floating upon the breast of the jeweled sea, a barge—gay with silken draperies, flowers and the music of many blades cleaving the waves.

Upon a golden couch lies a softly clad nymph. Sapphire are her eyes, alabaster her arms, coral tinges her mouth and pearls gleam, as the sun warms and bathes her in its rays.

177

So motionless she lies that one might think it a magical statue carven by a master hand—only, in the eyes gleams a force which keeps at regular beats the play of the blades and sends the craft to the port desired.

Supporting herself on one arm, she raises high the other and points to a gleaming palace by the water's edge, and with a quicker rhythm the barge sweeps over the water and reaches the landing.

It is a palace of dreams which appears to be holding within its walls the design of Aspiration.

Alighting from the barge, the nymph seems to float through the air, so lightly does she glide over the earth, and enters the palace.

In the entrance hall she hesitates and looks—from the left, where Music beckons, to the right, where Art smiles, and then stands and gazes at a closed door. It is simple in design and quite plain and ordinary compared to the rest of the palace, but unlike all the other doors, which stand open, this is tightly closed. On looking closer, over the portal can be seen in infinitesimal letters, the words Knowledge, Wisdom, Power.

In front of this door sits a figure wrapped in flowing garments. Hesitatingly, the nymph approaches, and addresses the figure in accents which are full of sweetness and yet are throbbing with will and determination.

"I would enter. Open the door for me."

"By what right do you issue that command?" asks the custodian.

"The right of Desire. Is that not sufficient?"

"Nay! not here. The other rooms may be entered and dwelt in by that alone, but this opens its doors only to aspiration for Qualities, for it is that knowledge only which can be gained within."

"Qualities! What are they? I tell you I will enter! You may sit there forever, if you will, but I shall pass you."

"Gladly will I stand aside for you when you are able to give me the pass-word which unlocks the door," replied its keeper.

"And where shall I purchase that word? No price is beyond me."

"There is no price. It is just a little word. Seek it diligently and you will find."

With a gesture of disdain the nymph swept past and entered the rooms, first to the left and then to the right, and then coming again to the closed door, seated herself and said:

"I WILL enter! No matter how long I must remain. What is the use of this palace to me, if that room

is closed? I will have none of it! I
command you to open the door."

But the figure remained motionless, and finally, wearying of the silence , the nymph approached and
touched the sleeve of the garment—
but, alas! it gave no response, for it
was stone.

II.

TODAY

Lying within the embrace of many
pillows was a woman, her eyes fixed
upon the sea, which rolled and tum-
bled below her making a very sym-
phony of sound.

Her eyes travelled slowly to the
horizon, then back to the book which
lay upon her lap. Picking it up she
commenced to read:

"Lying within each and every soul
is the seed which contains the memory of all past achievements, all past

desires, like a pure crystal which reflects all within its surface. Just as the crystal will reflect blurred pictures when it is marred by ill usage, so this seed fails to give the perfect flower of knowledge when it has met with neglect. To give it warmth will bring to view all its possibilities, all its loveliness.

"Make a search for that seed within you which contains all memories. Review each and every event by pouring upon it the sunshine of understanding and searching. Look within and "Know Thyself."

At this the woman put down her book and once again her gaze wandered to the horizon and within her eyes came a gleam—gazing intently —without movement.

One watching her would have said she saw something upon that sea, which stretched before her.

With a swift movement she slips

from her pillows, and with wide open
eyes, exclaims:

"The door—the same one of my
dreams."

Entranced, she remains motionless
until a sudden gust of wind picks up
her book and flings it at her feet.

Stooping, she picks it up, and then,
as her eyes scan the page, there is a
sudden tenseness of the body, as she
reads:—

"The key to the 'Temple of Knowledge' lies within each soul and he
who seeks, from the heart, shall find.
To knock imperiously will summon
the guardians, but to reach the inner
chamber it is necessary to enter first
into the closet of your own soul.

There, in a neglected corner, will
be the golden key. It will be in need
of burnishing, perhaps—hidden as it
has been all these years, but just a
little effort will bring out its brilliancy. Take it in your hands, rever-

ently, for it is fragile, as well as pure, and place it next to your heart. Keep it there until you can feel the warmth radiating from it, through your entire being. Then, and then only, is it ready for use, for it is then a Master Key and can unlock any door."

With a sudden exclamation, the book is clasped more closely, and a light of understanding breaks over her face.

"So simple! And I have searched so long!—Just love!"

III.

THE REAPING

In the streets flags are waving and banners unfurled to the breeze, while along the edges are eager, strained faces, watching.

With a shout, the cry rings out, "They are coming!" and then in the distance is heard the sound of music and the tramping of many feet, all in unison.

Gradually the marchers make their way past the waiting throngs, and as they pass, each head is raised in wonderment, and then reverently bowed, for, arm in arm march the Nations of the World,—all united in a common bond and no longer enemies, for at their head moves a tiny child, carrying in its hands a wee banner, but of mighty import,—for on it in letters of gold is

"The Ruler of all the World"

"LOVE"

Action—Reaction

Action—Reaction

ACTION

VILLAGE nestling among the pines. Only the buzz of insects and hum of bees, together with the accompaniment of rustling branches, breaks the silence.

All is peace and harmony.

Hark!

From afar sounds a discordant blatant note. Nearer it comes, ever growing harsher, until at last, at the end of the street is seen a mounted horseman, with a bugle at his lips. With one final blast he summons all the peaceful souls, who crowd about him. He watches them, as they gather, with an appraising eye, and then with uplifted hand commands silence.

"All men and boys past the age of twelve follow me.

"In the name of the Law you must obey! Come!"

Raising his bugle, once more he shatters the peace of that little hamlet and moves on, followed in silence by all the men and boys over twelve.

No sound but that of moving feet can be heard. No tears, no lamentations from the stricken statues left behind.

The hush of even-tide—
The drone of insects—
The hum of bees—
The swaying of branches,
Thrilled by the breeze—

and silence once more descends upon the street

Furroughed ground—
Booming guns—
Shrieking shells—
Smoke-laden air—

Young, old-men boys, automatons of
men, ply their trade at the command
"By order of the Law!   Obey!"

Daylight passes—
The hues of even-tide caress,
And speak of rest,

but the command rings out:
            "Forward! Attack!"

Night comes forth
With gleaming mantle,
And lays it over all that remains—
Furroughed ground!

REACTION

A bugle sounds in a hamlet town, and streaming forth come stricken souls, who with outstretched arms go forth to meet that straggling band which passes through the street—but they pay no heed.

Luminous are their faces, radiant their robes, as they gaze straight ahead, with never a look to the right or the left.

> Morning breezes—
> Buzz of insects
> Hum of bees—
> Branches bending
> To the breeze.

A Vision

A Vision

N the far distant East gleams a light—faint but effulgent, and as I watch it moves slowly, majestically, westward.

Still I gaze, and watch it ever going higher, moving more swiftly, and growing ever brighter and larger.

Still I gaze:

Swifter becomes its movement, more dazzling its light, and lo! from what seemed a speck when I first gazed upon that light, has grown a golden bird with outstretched wings gleaming and sending showers of golden radiance with each movement.

Westward it moves, ever expanding, ever more dazzling, until at last all the face of the world has been showered with the glimmering gold from its wings.

Still I gaze:

High in the heavens is motionless this wonderful golden bird—then, slowly, with scarcely moving pinions it descends, and with a final quiver takes under the shelter of its mighty wings a world of sorrow.

Still I gaze:

No movement, but ever the light increasing and dazzling in brilliancy and beauty.

Still I gaze:

A flutter—an unfolding of the mighty pinions and then a swift flight upwards—ever swifter—ever higher, until at last all sight of its wonder is lost.

Then I gaze where it rested, and behold! a new earth of dazzling gold and everywhere gleaming lights of rainbow tints

Then I muse:

And from out of the silence comes a voice:

"Thus will the world appear when Peace has folded it within its wings, and Love shines out from each and every window."